D1095866

KIDS' SPORTS STORIES

FIGURE SKATING FEARS

by Cari Meister

illustrated by Alex Patrick

PICTURE WINDOW BOOKS
a capstone imprint

Published by Picture Window Books, an imprint of Capstone
1710 Roe Crest Drive, North Mankato, Minnesota 56003
capstonepub.com

Library of Congress Cataloging-in-Publication Data
is available on the Library of Congress website.
ISBN 9781663909428 (hardcover)
ISBN 9781663921253 (paperback)
ISBN 9781663909398 (ebook PDF)

Summary: Raven is excited for the figure skating competition. She's been working hard on her lunge, and she wants to get it exactly right! But there's just one problem—Raven gets very nervous on competition days! She's been too nervous to compete before. This time, will she be able to overcome her fears?

Designer: Tracy Davies

Printed and bound in the USA. 4270

TABLE OF CONTENTS

Glossary

 **ice rink**—a place where ice is made smooth for skating

 **lunge**—a figure skating move where you bend the skating knee and put your free leg behind your body

 **routine**—a planned set of moves for a performance

 **skate guards**—pieces of plastic that go over skate blades to protect them

 **toe loop**—a simple figure skating jump where you use the tip of the back skate to push off to jump

Chapter 1

NO CLASS

Raven set her skate bag down by the door. "Let's go in ten minutes," she called.

Mom came in from the kitchen. "Coach Jen just called," she said. "Practice is canceled. The **ice rink** is closed."

"Why?" asked Raven.

"The storm is getting worse," said Mom.
Raven ran to the window. Snow was
coming down hard.

"But I need to practice," said Raven.
"The competition is in two weeks. I need to
get better at my **lunge**!"

Mom stroked Raven's long, black hair.
"I know," she said. "But there's not
anything you can do about the weather."

"I know," said Raven. "But I was feeling
really good about this competition. I really
want to do it."

Raven was a great skater. But she got very nervous before competitions. She would always show up, but when she walked near the ice, she would freeze with fear. Raven always ran to the car before it was her turn.

Chapter 2

PRACTICE MAKES ALMOST PERFECT

The next week, Raven went to practice. She pulled back her hair. She laced her skates. Then she took off her **skate guards**.

"I can't believe the competition is on Saturday!" said Kaiya.

Micah looked up. "I know, right?"

"Raven?" asked Kaiya. "Are you going to compete this time?"

Raven nodded.

"For real?" asked Kaiya.

Micah interrupted. "Raven, you'll do great! Your lunge is looking good!"

Raven smiled. "Thanks."

Coach Jen skated up to the bench. "Ready?" she asked. "Let's get to it! I want to see your **routines** from beginning to end. Then you can practice parts that need work. Sound good?"

Micah, Kaiya, and Raven nodded.

"Great!" said Jen. "Hit the ice!"

After they warmed
up, Kaiya did her
routine. Although
she fell a couple
of times, her form
looked great.

"Nice work,"
said Jen. "Just work on
landing that **toe loop**,
and you will do fine."

Micah went next.

"He looks
good," said
Raven. "And
he looks so
confident!
Doesn't he worry
that he will fall?"

Coach Jen smiled. "You look good skating too, Raven. You just need to tell yourself that. Stop focusing on what can go wrong. Don't worry about falling."

Raven nodded. But it wasn't that easy. She *always* worried about falling.

"You're up, Raven," said Coach Jen. "You've got this!"

Raven skated onto the ice. The first part of her routine was almost perfect. Then it was time for the lunge. Raven looked at Jen. Jen nodded. Raven went into the lunge and didn't fall!

Jen clapped. "That's it!" she said.
"Do your routine on Saturday just like
that. And if you fall that's okay too."

Chapter 3
COLD FEET

Finally, the big day arrived. "Are you ready?" asked Mom.

"Yes!" said Raven. Raven did feel ready. Her hair was done. She had on a new skating costume.

"I can do this!" she said.

"That's the spirit!" said Mom.

But when they arrived at the ice rink, Raven's stomach turned.

Raven went to the locker room. Coach Jen was there. She said something, but Raven couldn't focus. Her hands started to sweat. Her heart raced.

"I'll be right back," she said.

Raven ran out and bumped into Micah.

"Sorry," said Raven.

"No problem," he said. "Are you okay?"

Raven shook her head no. She looked at her shoes.

"You don't have to do this," Micah said. "Skating is for fun."

"But I want to do it," said Raven. "I just get so scared."

"Scared to fall?" Micah asked.

Raven nodded.

"Well, I fall all the time at competitions," Micah said.

"Really?" asked Raven. She didn't know that. She had never stayed to watch.

"Yes," said Micah. "It's not a big deal. Everyone falls. And think about it this way. If you fall today, you will still go home knowing you did the competition."

"That's true," said Raven. "So I just have to do it."

"If you want," said Micah.

"I do!" said Raven.

"Here's something else," said Micah.
"It helps me. It may help you. Before I go
onto the ice, I close my eyes. Then I take
three deep, calming breaths. I breathe in
slowly through my nose. Then I breathe
out slowly through my mouth."

Raven nodded. "I'll try that."

Raven waited on the bench until she was called. Then, she did three deep, calming breaths and skated out onto the ice. What happened next was a blur. She did remember falling once, but it wasn't a big deal.

When she was done, she took a bow and skated off the ice.

Micah and Kaiya smiled. They cheered.

Coach Jen gave her a hug. "You did it!"
she said.

Raven smiled. "I did!" she said.
"I finally did it!"

KEEP CALM!

Do you get nervous before a competition?

Some foods can help you feel calmer.
Try one of these snacks before a big event.

- bananas in yogurt
- a handful of nuts
- oatmeal

You can also try to take calming breaths.

- Take a slow, deep breath through your nose.
- Hold your breath for five seconds.
- Open your mouth and slowly breathe out.
- Repeat two more times.

REPLAY IT

Take another look at this illustration. How do you think Raven felt when she got to the ice rink? Have you ever felt nervous before an event?

Now pretend you are Raven. Write a thank-you note to Micah for being such a supportive friend.

ABOUT THE AUTHOR

Cari Meister is the author of more than 100 books for children, including the Fairy Hill series and the Tiny series. She lives with her family in Vail, Colorado. She enjoys yoga, horseback riding, and skiing. You can visit her online at www.carimeister.com.

ABOUT THE ILLUSTRATOR

Alex Patrick was born in the Kentish town of Dartford in the southeast of England. He has been drawing for as long as he can remember. His life-long love for cartoons, picture books, and comics has shaped him into the passionate children's illustrator he is today. Alex loves creating original characters. He brings an element of fun and humor to each of his illustrations and is often found laughing to himself as he draws.